D1463552

WHICH WAY, WENDY?

by Tennant Redbank
illustrated by Rebecca Thornburgh

Kane Press, Inc.
New York

Library of Congress Cataloging-in-Publication Data

Redbank, Tennant.
  Which way, Wendy? / by Tennant Redbank ; illustrated by Rebecca Thornburgh.
    p. cm. — (Social studies connects)
  "Geography - grades: 1–3."
  Summary: To return a lost map to its owners, Wendy must learn how
to follow it.
  ISBN 1-57565-147-5 (pbk. : alk. paper)
  [1. Lost and found possessions—Fiction. 2. Map reading—Fiction.]
I. Thornburgh, Rebecca McKillip, ill. II. Title. III. Series.
  PZ7.D943Wj 2005
  [Fic]—dc22
                                    2004016960

10 9 8 7 6 5 4 3 2 1

First published in the United States of America in 2005 by Kane Press, Inc.
Printed in Hong Kong.

Social Studies Connects is a trademark of Kane Press, Inc.

Book Design: Edward Miller

www.kanepress.com

I tiptoe up to the clubhouse. I ignore the big sign
that says PRIVATE and put my ear against the door.

The kids inside are the Kellys and the Dunns—
cousins and brothers and sisters and best friends.
They always stick together, and they always have fun.

3

I'd better explain. I never used to spy on anyone. But I'm new in town. And I have no one to hang out with—no brother or sister or cousin. And no best friend.

If only I were a Kelly or a Dunn. Then I could be in their club!

I peek through the window. Tom is unfolding
something. A map!

"Hey, guys!" Tom sounds excited. "Remember I
told you how Dad and I found a secret
cave last week? Well, Dad said it was okay
for us to check it out by ourselves! He
even gave me a map to help us get there."

"Cool!" says Brian.

A **map** is a picture
of a place as seen
from above. It's a
bird's-eye view!

Tom shows the map to the other kids. "First we have to go to the high school," he says. "Then we cross the soccer field and head for the trees. After that, it gets sort of tricky. There's a stream, and a stone wall, and a funny-looking tree . . . But Dad marked the map to show the way."

"Wow!" Colleen says. "Let's go!"

"I don't know," Mickey grumbles.
"I feel hot. I think I have a fever.
Maybe it's scarlet fever! Do I look
scarlet to you?"

Everyone laughs. I smile, too.

"Mickey, you always think you're sick," says Brian.

"You're hot because it's summer," Brenda says.

"Come on. It'll be fun!"

Most maps have a **compass rose**. It shows which direction is north on the map. It usually shows east, west, and south, too.

Uh-oh. They're leaving!
I dart behind a tree. Seconds
later, the Kellys and the Dunns come
out, still laughing and talking. Their voices fade as
they walk away. The last thing I hear is Mickey saying,
"My big toe hurts. I hope it's not far to the cave."
A cave—that really sounds like fun.

I see something on the path. The map! Tom must have dropped it. I run and pick it up.

I know what I'll do! I'll follow the map until I catch up to them. Then I'll give it back.

I'll be a hero!

DID YOU KNOW?
Maps have been around for thousands of years. Even long ago, people needed to know how to get from one place to another.

There's a problem. I've never used a map before, and I sure don't know my way around town. But how hard can it be to read a map?

I take a good look at it. There are lots of lines and squares and colors and tiny pictures. What do they all mean? Then I see "MAP KEY" in big letters.

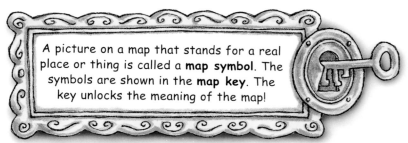

A picture on a map that stands for a real place or thing is called a **map symbol**. The symbols are shown in the **map key**. The key unlocks the meaning of the map!

Ah-ha! The key tells what the tiny pictures stand for. A mailbox means the post office. A book stands for the library. A cupcake stands for the bakery. Now it all makes sense! I hurry after the Kellys and the Dunns.

MAP KEY

—— Streets	🖂 Post Office	🛡 Police Station
〰 Stream	🏛 Town Hall	🔺 Fire Station
▦ Bridge	🏫 High School	📖 Library
🚶 Hiking Trail	🏫 Elementary School	Ⓗ Hospital
🧁 Bakery	⚽ Soccer Field	⚾ Baseball Field
🌳 Park		

library

akery

I go past the library. And there's the bakery—just where the map said it would be! After I pass it, I turn right.

I follow Berry Street until I come to the high school. Then I cut through the soccer field and head for the hiking trail.

I see lots of hikers, but no Kellys, no Dunns.

High
School

Soccer
Field

Hiking
Trail

I come to the stream. There's a bridge made of logs and boards. I cross it. That's fun. It's so fun, I go back and cross it again!

The cave can't be far now. But I still don't see the Kellys or the Dunns. Then I hear a voice. It's Tom!

"It must be around here somewhere," Tom is saying.

"I can't believe you lost the map!" Colleen snaps.

"I should have carried it," Brian says.

"Can't anybody remember where we go after we cross the stream?" asks Brenda.

"I'm dizzy," Mickey groans. "Maybe I have malaria!"

DID YOU KNOW?
On a map, watery places—ponds, rivers, oceans—are usually shown in blue.

I want to give the map back—but they might be mad at me. I took it, and it wasn't mine. Maybe I'll just sneak away . . .

Oh, no! Brenda has spotted me!

"Look! It's that new girl, Wendy!" says Brenda. "Hi!" I call out brightly. "I found your map and followed it to catch up with you. I figured you might need it."

"We sure do!" Tom says. "We're trying to find a really cool cave. But we can't remember the directions." He checks the map.

"The wall!" says Tom. "I forgot about turning off the trail at the stone wall!"

"It's right back there," I say.

We all start walking.

And this time the Kellys and the Dunns follow *me!*

Stone
Wall

We turn right at the wall and head down an old curvy path.

"I feel itchy," Mickey says. "I hope it isn't poison ivy."

Funny
Tree

We pass the funny-looking tree. It's easy to spot.

Tom's dad drew his own map symbols for the stone wall and the funny tree.

"There it is!" I yell. "The cave!"

It's just as great as I thought it would be. The floor feels cool and damp. The walls sparkle with shiny stones. Everybody starts exploring— everybody but Mickey, that is.

"I'm not going in there!" he says. "Damp places give you whooping cough!"

Nobody tries to change Mickey's mind. We're having too much fun.

A minute later, we hear a scream.

"Aaaahhhhh!" Mickey cries. "It got me!"

We all dash outside. Mickey's standing by a blackberry bush and rubbing his arm.

"What's wrong this time?" Colleen asks.

Mickey holds out his arm. "A bee came right at me! I dodged to the left. I dodged to the right. I jumped back and fell into the bush. I got stabbed by a HUGE thorn!"

"That little red scratch there?" Brian asks.

Mickey nods. "Yes!" he groans. "I'm losing blood! I—feel—faint!"

"Mickey, it's only a scratch," Colleen says. "But we should wash it out."

"Where?" Brian asks. "The stream?"

"The hospital!" Mickey moans. "The emergency room!"

"You don't go to the emergency room for a scratch," says Tom.

"I had a check-up with Dr. Biddle last week," I say. "We could go to his office."

Mickey looks at me like I'm the smartest person in the universe. "Can we?" he asks.

"Oh, I guess so," says Brenda. "But how do we get there from here?"

"We can follow the map," I say.

"There's no symbol for a doctor's office, Wendy," says Tom.

"Isn't his office next to the hospital?" I ask.

"Yes!" Tom says. "And there *is* a symbol for *that!*"

Tom and I lead the way.
"No, I won't carry you," Colleen tells Mickey.
"The scratch is on your arm. Your legs still work!"

Finally we're at Dr. Biddle's office. It's not the emergency room, but Mickey is excited to be there. "Look at all the medicine!" he says. "And those bandages—they're great!"

Dr. Biddle washes the scratch and puts a bandage on it. "You'll be fine now," he tells Mickey.

"I'm not so sure," says Mickey. "This morning I felt like I had scarlet fever. You get it from germs."

"That's right, Mickey." Dr. Biddle chuckles. "You seem to know a lot about medicine. Maybe you'll be a doctor someday."

All the way back to the clubhouse Mickey keeps saying, "Doctor. Doctor Mickey Dunn. Mickey Dunn, M.D. Doctor Mickey Dunn, M.D."

"Sounds good to me," says Brian.

I stop outside the clubhouse door.

"Here's your map, Tom." I turn to go home.

"You *can't* go, Wendy," says Mickey. "You saved my life!"

"You're part of our club now," Colleen tells me. "You're an honorary Kelly."

"No way!" Brenda says. "She's a Dunn!"

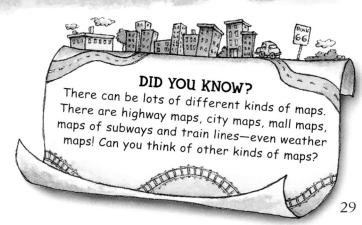

DID YOU KNOW?
There can be lots of different kinds of maps. There are highway maps, city maps, mall maps, maps of subways and train lines—even weather maps! Can you think of other kinds of maps?

I can't stop smiling. This morning I had nobody to hang out with.

Now I feel like I have brothers and sisters and cousins—and five brand new best friends!

I understand map symbols!

MAKING CONNECTIONS

Lots of maps use symbols to stand for places. Some symbols look exactly like what they represent—and some don't! On Wendy's map, the symbol for the Town Hall looks like a real building. But the symbol for the post office is just a mailbox.

If you want to figure out map symbols, just remember—the map key is your key to success!

Look Back

- Look at the map on page 11. When Wendy follows the trail past the library, what does she pass next? Now look at the illustration on page 12. Were you right?
- Suppose the Kellys and Dunns want to go to the baseball field. If they start out from the clubhouse, what places will they pass? (Hint: They take the shortest route.)

Try This!

These map symbols are all mixed up. Can you match each symbol to the place it stands for?

PLACE	MAP SYMBOLS
1. I Scream for Ice Cream Parlor	A.
2. Jolly Lollipop Shoppe	B.
3. Pet Paradise	C.
4. Bake-A-Cakery	D.
5. Haircut Hut	E.
6. Bouncing Baby Toys	F.

Answers: 1. B, 2. E, 3. D, 4. C, 5. F, 6. A

32